Publisher's Note: This is a work of fiction. Names, characters, places, and incidents are a product of the author's imagination. Locales and public names are sometimes used for atmospheric purposes. Any resemblance to actual people, living or dead, or to businesses, companies, events, institutions, or locales is coincidental.

Edited by Aquila Editing

Cover Designer: Cormar Covers

❀ Created with Vellum

SECRET BABY *on* BOARD

ABBY KNOX

Summary

Vanessa

I've finally landed my dream job, and I intend to celebrate that before I ship out tomorrow. When I meet the handsome Ian at the hotel bar, a night of passion turns into something unexpected. I shouldn't let myself catch feelings. However Ian and I click so well, he leaves his mark on me. Unfortunately, I'm so caught up in our short time together that I make a series of life-changing mistakes, and no way to reach him. I may be the organized chief stew on the outside, but inside, I'm an absolute mess.

Ian

I don't do one-night stands. After the most incredible night of my life with Vanessa, I want more. I want every night to be with her and nobody else. Unfortunately, a family emergency pulls me back home to the States, and I have no way to reach Vanessa on the yacht where she works. That is, until a dubious opportunity falls in my lap that helps me to track her down. I don't care who I have to pay, I have to find her. Once I have her back in my arms, though, something feels off. There's something distant about her, and I aim to find out what's going on. We are meant to be together and there won't be any distance, any secrets, or any barrier between us ever again.

Chapter One

Vanessa

I'M FEELING MYSELF TODAY.

That's the only explanation for me being daring enough to grace this posh hotel bar with my awkward Midwestern presence.

I am full to the brim with splurging on myself for the first time in a long time.

And now, all that overconfidence has led me to this moment. I am about to have a consequence-free night with a man so beautiful I am questioning my entire skincare regime.

"Tell me more about this farm of yours, Vanessa?" Ian leans sideways, his elbow on the bar. He's not pushing into my personal space, I note. Just fully present, facing me.

I snort in the most unattractive way possible and cover my mouth with my hand. His smile only grows wider, his golden-brown eyes trained on me.

The server brings me my third vodka soda of the night.

The staff at this Monte Carlo have been achingly polite to me, a nobody who has spent her week bumping and bumbling around the playground of the fabulously tanned wealthy. There's no way I would try to rub elbows with the elite of the elite on a typical lag between charters. I am a practical girl who stays in hostels and far-flung affordable rentals whenever there's no time to go home to Indiana to see my brother.

But now? I deserve to celebrate my good news. I nailed my job interview with the staffing agency. Tomorrow, I ship off as a chief stewardess aboard a 150-foot yacht in the Mediterranean.

"It's not *my* farm," I correct Ian, not wanting him to think I'm some kind of wealthy landowner. "It was my great-granddad's." I realize most people might try to lie to impress. I do the opposite. I downplay everything, sometimes to my own detriment. My brother runs the dairy, and both our names are on the deed by way of inheritance. But I hardly feel I deserve it, as others before me made it what it is today.

"And you've milked the cows?"

I nod and sip my drink, preferring a fruity cocktail, but I report to the dock at eight a.m., and I have to look my best. As much as I love sugar, it gives me under-eye bags and terrible hangovers.

"Yes," I reply. "Many times."

"Show me how."

I cock my head and laugh. "Show you? I don't know what you mean. You got a cow in your pocket or something for me to demonstrate on?"

He chuckles and explains himself, mimicking in the air with his hands what he thinks milking a cow looks like. He resembles a cartoon.

Laughing, I inform him of the bad news. "I'm so sorry,

Ian, but the cows and I discussed it, and we're going to have to let you go."

He laughs with his whole body, tossing his head back. I didn't think it was that funny, but he may be slightly tipsy. We both are.

"There goes my farmhand career," he says, shaking his fist at the heavens.

I think I like this man.

I laugh again. "Unless you want to get kicked in the head. Mostly we just disinfect the teat, then attach the milking machines."

He repeats the word back to me in shock. "Machines? Sorry, I know nothing about farms."

Is this man never going to respond to me with a "Well, actually"? Is this man real? Not once tonight has he tried spouting off on something I know more about, which might be a record. I don't know; the bar is pretty low based on most men I've dated. Clearly, I've picked the wrong ones. Too bad that Ian is just a one-night stand, and I'll never see him again come morning.

"Where did you say you were from?"

He winces. "Chicago."

I burst out laughing. "Illinois is mostly farmland."

Ian laughs again. "Yes, but my family is in the hotel chain business. I grew up traveling all over, so I know nothing about anything else. I'm fact I'm here overseeing a renovation project of one of our latest acquisitions."

I smile. "A lifelong world traveler. That explains why I can't place your accent," I say.

It's true. Ian articulates slowly, with careful diction and impeccable grammar. Most people from my little town in northern Indiana would feel put off by his proper way of speaking but not me. My mom and dad were both schoolteachers, and I knew better than to use double negatives.

He smiles back, and I notice his eyes drift down to my lips. "That must be why I was drawn to you. When I heard you order that drink, I needed to know you. You reminded me of…home."

The words slide down like warm honey that spreads from my middle out to my fingertips. I feel caressed. Everywhere.

The conversation drifts into the region of college basketball and who makes the best Italian beef sandwich.

"Hoosiers aren't supposed to know this stuff," Ian teases.

"Get over it, buddy," I retort. "We've got all the same TV stations, the same pizza. But our taxes are lower."

He winces, and his hand goes to one side of his ribcage as if I've just shot him with an arrow.

My eyes rake down, landing on his watch, and I go in for the kill. "You do know what taxes are, right? It's what us suckers cough up to make sure guys like you don't take your proverbial football and relocate your businesses elsewhere."

Liquid courage from the vodka? Maybe, but if I'm going to spend this night with a rich guy, he'd better be worth fucking. Guys of less prestige than this man have spat out misogynist slurs at me for less of an offense than this.

"Fair," he says, his eyes now traveling down to my collarbone, visible in the spaghetti strap slip of a dress. I blush, knowing that this same Forever 21 clearance-sale purchase has been my go-to party dress for the past ten years. That this orange rayon thing is in such good shape has more to do with how seldom I go out to party and less to do with what I've learned about laundry in the bowels of yachts over the years. I examine the French stitching of his white shirt, which is less impressive than the corded forearms revealed by his rolled-up sleeves. His watch glints at me. I've learned many things about how this half of the world lives throughout my years in yachting, and that is an extremely rare Paul Newman Rolex Daytona. It is the sexiest watch ever made, made sexier even by the wearer.

"But," he continues, "there's no one vacationing here that isn't obscenely wealthy, so I don't know what you think you'll find while going out at night in Monte Carlo."

I should bristle at this, but for some reason, I don't. Ian's tone is more of a challenge than a critique, and I like it.

"Not looking for a sugar daddy, if that's what you mean."

This catches him off-guard. "Oh no. Oh my god. I didn't mean that. I only meant…."

I reach over and rest a hand on his forearm. The fine hairs are soft under my touch, and his skin is warm. "Relax. I just wanted to see you squirm, Ian."

Me saying his name softly does something to him. He takes a moment before he speaks, and I see a barely restrained predator behind his eyes. He chews on his lip. He wants something, and he's debating whether or not to come right out and ask for it.

Throwing me for a loop, he asks, "Wanna see my scar?"

I respond immediately. "I have never said no to that question and will never," I declare, my expression probably a little too hungry.

He props his foot on the barstool and rolls up his pant leg. A curved line, about five shades paler than the rest of him, stretches from below his knee to his ankle.

"What is that?"

"Shark bite."

I gasp. "What the fuck, dude? You're supposed to swim away from their mouths."

Laughing along with me, he explains what happened. "I was on a fishing boat in the Gulf of Mexico. While diving under to deal with a tangled anchor chain, the son of a bitch got me."

Eyes wide, I ask, "May I touch it?"

"Please do. I mean, yes, you may."

I run my fingertips over the scar, tracing the curve up to his knee and back down to where his muscled calf meets his ankle. I could be mistaken, but I think I hear a groan coming from him. A low, indistinct rumble in response to my touch. Feeling braver, I gingerly turn his leg to take in the entire scope of the injury.

"How long ago?"

"About five years."

I look up and study his face again, the same face I've been staring at for an hour. He's so young looking. "How old were you when you were working on a boat?"

"I was 25 at the time."

Something about his story doesn't add up. "Why would you be a fisherman when your family has hotel chain money?"

Ian moves his foot off the barstool and rights himself. He shrugs like it should be obvious. "I wanted to see other shit. Why do you work on yachts if you have a farm and family back home? It's a lonely lifestyle."

Smirking, I reply, "I wanted to see other shit."

He huffs out a short laugh and finally loses the leash on his tether.

"Would you like to go somewhere private right now? With me?"

I'm almost relieved that he's asked me. I don't know how much longer I can keep up the banter.

Ian moves like liquid down the elegantly appointed hallway, his hand on my bare lower back. He smoothly opens the door to his suite and gestures for me to enter first.

I deserve this. Good things are coming to me.

I barely contain the smirk as I think, Oh, things are about to come, all right.

Chapter Two

Ian

"WAIT. BEFORE WE DO THIS," Vanessa asks, sitting on the edge of the bed and crossing her legs to massage the inside of her ankle, "I need to know. Cubs or Sox?"

This is a tricky question.

I almost didn't hear it because I was staring at her ankle. And at the delicious underside of her thigh, visible with her legs crossed like that.

"Cubs."

She makes a noise like a game show buzzer. "Wrong!"

I can't believe cross-town rivals have found each other on this side of the Atlantic and that we're considering doing what we're about to do.

"Would you let a Cubs fan make it worth your while?"

Looking a little confused, she's about to reply when I'm already on my knees, unbuckling and removing her five-inch heels.

"Oh," she says softly. And then "Oh," a little louder as

I slide in next to her on the bed. I take both of her legs with me and prop them in my lap so I can massage her feet and ankles.

Shyly, Vanessa tucks a lock of hair behind her ear. I watch the pink spread across her chest, her neck. I want to brush aside the wispy strands in front of her ear and taste her juicy little earlobe. I'd swallow that golden hoop and choke to death with my luck.

And somehow, this golden creature next to me is still turned on by me.

I keep massaging because she seems to enjoy it. At least, the soft moans and her head tilting back would indicate so. My cock twitches in response to Vanessa's supple, exposed neck. Her skin glows with some kind of shimmery lotion, hypnotizing me.

I lean forward, unable to keep my distance, wafting my breath across her collarbone. I inhale her scent. Something fresh and young and citrusy.

She gasps at the contact from the slight brush of my lips.

"I should have asked. May I kiss you, Vanessa?"

She lowers her gaze to me and smiles, leaning in. Our lips come together playfully at first. We softly tease each other between our slightly tipsy giggles and laughter.

"I'm surprised you didn't try To kiss me at the bar before inviting me back to your room. I could be awful at it, you don't know," she says, her gaze heated and challenging. Her forwardness revs my engines, and I go in for another kiss, slightly longer. A little wetter.

"Oh, I did want to. I just didn't want anyone to get turned on by watching us."

She huffs. "No one is getting turned on by watching us kiss. I'm a blundering idiot."

"Have you zero self-awareness? You're delightful. Sexy.

Funny. Fun to talk to. Beautiful. And that dress…I'm sorry to tell you this, but I cannot overemphasize the filthy thoughts that popped into my head. My goal from the very beginning was to whisk you away from the public eye because literally, no one in that bar could stop staring at you."

With her glossy lips parted as she stares at me, I have to use all the restraint in my arsenal. Softly, lightly, I brush my lips against hers. I want to kiss her so hard and take her down to the bed with me. Let us maul each other. But I want her wet and begging for it with her body and her words.

Vanessa's breath mingles with mine as our lips feather against each other. My tongue slides gently over her bottom lip. She tastes like summer: coconut and lime. I think of basking in the sunshine with her on a hot day at the beach. A nude beach. The brief fantasy pops like a balloon at the thought of anyone else seeing her naked. What is this possessiveness pouring out of me? This is not who I am; what has she done to me?

Noticing her sighs, feeling her press closer, I pull back again. She looks at me with surprise. The small glimpse of her pink tongue inside her open mouth might send me into orbit.

"Well? Am I that bad at kissing or…?" Her words demand a clear answer that I give with my whole self. The teasing is over. My lips capture hers, my hands cease their massaging of her ankles, and I cup her face. I need more, and I can't hold back no matter how much I enjoy the torment. As we kiss, I slide my tongue over her lip again, and she opens her mouth for me. The tangle of tongues is warm and more intoxicating than gin and tonics. Everything fades away. The room, the thoughts of her shipping out tomorrow. The sad family news I know is looming from back home in Chicago. We have this moment, and nothing else is promised.

My left hand wanders down to cup her breast, soft and full in my hand. Her nipple peaks at the contact. The soft gasp from Vanessa causes me to ease away, only slightly. The tight ache in my cock goes from a nuisance to nearly unbearable at what I see. Her eyes are still closed, and she lets out a low whimper as I softly squeeze and caress her breast.

"Ian," she whispers.

"I want you, sweetheart. So fucking bad right now."

Her eyes open, her nostrils flare. She nods, fisting my shirt and pulling me down to the mattress with her.

The kissing intensifies, both of us demanding more from the other. My hand skims over Vanessa's hip as she lies on her side, hiking up the hem as my fingers catch on the delicate fabric.

She inhales sharply, and I freeze.

"Vanessa. Talk to me. I can wait. You can think about it, and if you still want to see me on your day off, I'll meet you. Anywhere. We can even wait until your charter season ends. We don't have to do anything you don't want to."

Her laugh catches me off-guard. "Oh. No, I'm gonna fuck you tonight," she says, biting sharply on my lip.

Is it possible for my cock to grow another three inches just from those words? From the feral contact of those teeth? I don't know if it's possible, but that's how she makes me feel. Hornier and hornier from one moment to the next.

With those words, she pushes me onto my back and mounts me like a steed, slipping off her dress and chucking it across the room.

She's bare to me except for a lacy, barely-there set of red panties.

"I just need to be on top, so I don't pass out. You good?"

"Hell yeah, girl."

I hook my finger in the elastic and raise an eyebrow. "I'll be honest, there is something I've always wanted to try…."

"Do it, Ian," she demands.

"I don't want to hurt you."

"Listen, young man, I bought these for the stretch. Do it." She comes up on her knees.

With the heat in my loins leading the way, I grip them in my thick fingers and tug hard. They rip easily, and I toss them aside.

I pull her down to me because I need more kissing. More skin to skin, more touching and groping and grabbing and grazing. While she's on top of me, kissing me, I take one breast in my hand, softly kneading it.

My other hand slides down between her legs. She's so wet already, but I have to make sure she's ready to take me.

I scrape the side of my hand through her folds, and her breath hitches. She follows this with a moan into my mouth.

"Ian, oh god. Yes."

I'm so overcome I barely make a grunt in response.

She drags the tip of her tongue over my bottom lip. "Come on. Don't tell me those juicy lips don't know how to talk dirty?"

Vanessa licks the stubble on my neck, and a floodgate opens up.

"Do you know what I was thinking about when I saw you in the bar? Do you want to talk about dirty? If you knew, you'd slap me across the face."

"Tell me. I want to know. I want to know all of it," she

breathes, skimming her hand down my chest and undoing my buttons.

As she talks, she grinds herself against my cock, which is now straining to be free of my trousers. I can feel her heat between her legs.

"I wanted you to smother me."

"That's a start," she says with a smirk.

"No, I'm serious. I want you to sit on my face. Smother me while you come so hard you drown me with your stickiness."

Vanessa's eyes flash wickedly. "Get ready."

I adjust on the bed so she can straddle my face and hold on to the headboard.

She lowers her pussy onto my face, but I still her hips. "No. You don't move a muscle. Let me."

"Oh…oh," she breathes.

I take control of her movements, guiding her up and down on my tongue.

She's more divine than I imagined. Better than champagne and juicier than the ripest grapes falling off the vine.

I drink her in, letting her juice run down my chin. I can't get enough.

What I said before was a lie. I didn't think about eating her pussy the second I saw her. What I thought about when I saw her was that I wanted her to be my wife. The second thought was about going downtown, sure.

Using my hands, I grind her against my mouth. I can feel her little clit harden against the pressure. I suck it into my mouth and let my tongue make a toy of it.

"Ian, oh my god. Yes!"

Lifting her up so I can breathe, I take advantage of this brief second to gaze at her gorgeous, wet pussy.

"Are you my dirty girl?"

"Yes, Ian."

"Come for me right now."

Delving deep and delivering another kiss to her clit, she finally lets go, coming with a loud gasp and a curse.

Gripping her tight, I swiftly move us around, so she's now under me.

"Ian!"

"My turn. You ready for the dicking?"

Vanessa laughs. "You're ridiculous. But yes. Now, please."

I swiftly unbuckle, shuffling off my trousers, shirt, and underwear.

I reach for the nightstand, where I keep the condoms, and she stays my hand.

For a moment, I'm taken aback. "Uh…"

"I have a diaphragm. It's all good."

"But you don't even know me."

"You're right. Are you clean? I've been tested. I'm all good."

"I'm clean. Are you sure?"

I'd love nothing more than to raw dog this girl without a second thought, let my passion take us away on a wave of pleasure. But the last thing I want is for her to catch something. Like a baby.

She nods and places a hand on my cock.

That's all the prompting I need, and I notch the tip inside, feeling her damp heat paint my skin.

I cover my cock in her juice, exploring her as I slick myself in her essence.

"Stop teasing me," she whines.

And then, I'm all the way in, stretching her out.

"Ian," she breathes. I love how she says my name, and I tell her so.

"Vanessa. Hold on to me. You're so damn tight I'm going to explode."

"You're so deep, Ian."

"Too deep?"

"No, never. Give me more; I want to feel you move inside me."

I pull out and root back inside her, and her hips lift off the mattress. In and out, I move over her and into her, thrusting and grunting. Vanessa's juicy lips open, her mouth slackens, her eyes pleading.

God, I want to keep doing this. Every night, every morning. Forever.

There's so much more I want to do, want to say, but we only have tonight.

I can't let myself think of how much it sucks that we only have tonight.

With another thrust into her, I blurt out decidedly not dirty words.

"What time do you shove off tomorrow?"

"What? Oh…eight a.m."

What the hell is wrong with me? Where is my stupid mouth taking me?

"Don't go," I say.

"What? I have to." Vanessa's eyes are wide and blinking.

"Don't go. Stay here. Let me take care of you."

"Ian."

I move back into her, noticing the muscles of her sex squeeze my dick. God, she's even tighter now, so tight I almost can't breathe. If I thought I wanted to die from asphyxiation between her thighs, I think now might be an even happier death.

I pull out again and slide in again, thrusting harder. "I know. It's crazy. But I want to see you again."

She bites her lip. "It's only a few months. We'll see each other again if the stars align."

It's a beautiful thought, randomly running into each other, sharing a drink, reminiscing about tonight. A lovely idea, and I hate it. I don't want that. I want Vanessa. I want her to not go out on a stupid boat. I want. I want... what do I want?

I want more of her.

I climb to my knees and hoist her legs up, pinning them against my shoulder, allowing me to thrust deeper, more thoroughly. It doesn't follow logic, but something preternatural in me thinks that maybe if I go deep enough, she'll understand. I'll leave a mark on her, leave something with her, plant my face in her memory, and she'll comprehend how strongly I feel for her.

I don't want her to give up her fabulous job. Not when she's so excited and worked so hard for it. But damn, I also want her to call in sick on her first day. Give me time to get everything squared away so that we can be together permanently when she comes back. That's what I want.

My release hits me like a load of bricks. I roar Vanessa's name as I surge into her, my seed bursting in a hot rush. My mind goes blank for those few seconds.

It's not until the rush passes and my blank brain recovers that I realize what sex with Vanessa has pulled out of me. More than just baby batter. She's pulled out all my hopes and dreams.

And, fuck me, she's leaving tomorrow.

Chapter Three

Vanessa

IAN IS GONE in the morning.

We had fun while it lasted. That's what I tell myself.

Rolling over to my side, I run my hands over the space where he slept.

I sit up, noticing the twinge between my legs, and smile.

Too bad that's the only mark he will leave on me.

How many hours has it been since we did the deed?

I know when we started, I think to myself, smiling dopily while I come to standing. My arms stretch wide over my head, and I let out a huge yawn, laughing about how I don't exactly know when we stopped having sex. In that case, I'd better leave my diaphragm in for now and toss it later today while I'm on the boat.

Just as I'm finishing the stretch, I feel something fall out of me. I freeze in horror.

There, on the floor, between my feet, is the little domed

silicone device. The only thing standing between me and
chances of an utterly life-changing circumstance.

Breathe, Vanessa. It's all gonna be okay. I'll just pop by
a pharmacy before I get to the boat. I reach down and
grab my diaphragm, and it's then that I see something else.
A note, folded in half. It must have fallen on the floor when
I'd scooted out of bed. I sit back down and unfold it,
reading Ian's inevitable goodbye letter.

Dear Vanessa.

*The plan was to wake you up with chocolate croissants and coffee
and make plans to reconnect after your charter. I'm so sorry, but there's
been a family emergency; I'm okay. Don't worry. But my sister's
husband is in stage 4 cancer, and I got the call I was dreading. Here's
my number. The room is on permanent reserve so take your time.
Please call or text when you can. Dammit, I should have asked for
your number, but I didn't want to wake you.*

Best,

Ian.

P.S. You snore.

P.S.S. It's a cute snore.

Damn.

I hate that he had a family emergency. I believe what
he wrote is true. Anyone invoking a cancer excuse with no
cancer will soon have karma to deal with.

I take my phone and the note and pad to the bathroom. What time is it, anyway? Gulping down some water
for my parched throat, I check my phone. The most epic
of spit takes splatters the bathroom mirror. I have to be on
the dock in 45 minutes! The yacht will leave promptly for
the tiny Mediterranean island of Austero to pick up our
first charter of the season.

You're not going to make it! says the negative gremlin who
lives permanently in my head.

I curl my fist into a ball and make my game face in the water-splashed mirror. "Oh yes, the fuck I am!"

I'll have to hurry. I'll have to skip my plans to go back to my room, take a luxurious shower, and do my hair. Instead, I throw on my dress and grab a pair of dubiously-clean-but-good-enough men's track shorts that I fish out from a laundry bag hanging on the bathroom door. I doubt Ian will care, but I'll text him later to let him know I'll send these back to him.

The sprint to my room takes longer than it should, as I have to dig around in my evening clutch for my room key because I'm such a spaz. When I'm finally inside, I have forty minutes. I grab my simple overnight bag, as my luggage for three months on the ship has already been delivered to the dock by now. Shit. I'll have to shower on the boat after my first shift. I hate this. This is what I get for manifesting a magical night.

I did get a magical night, but I failed to manifest a magical and leisurely morning.

Instead, I am running like a maniac through this fancy hotel, shouting for the concierge to please call for a cab. I hate running.

Ten minutes later, and bordering on total freak-out, I'm finally hurling myself into the back of a cab. "Quai Chicane!" I shout, and in my limited French I beg the driver to get me to that section of Port Hercule as fast as she can; then I ask, "Do you mind if I change?"

She says something I barely understand, but I get the gist with her shrug.

I wiggle out of my dress and Ian's track shorts in the back seat and don my underwear, fresh khaki shorts, a good bra, and a tee-shirt. The driver guns it through a red light and hangs a sharp left. I grip the head cushion in front of me for balance as the marina comes into view. No time to do nice hair, I fist it into a bun. We'll likely be cleaning the boat today, anyway, so there is no point in doing full hair and makeup, but I'd at least hoped to look sharp. I'm as presentable as I can expect, with a bit of toner spritzed on my puffy face, plus a quick dab of eyeliner, lip gloss, and deodorant.

We arrive at the dock at 7:59, and I'm almost sick with anxiety. I pay the cab, and she zooms away.

When I reach the gangplank, I'm sweating through my clothes. Lovely. I cast my eyes around frantically for a glimpse of the captain. Seeing no one, I exhale slowly and pull my nerves together, digging in my pocket for my phone to let my brother know I made it.

That's odd, I think. I then remember stuffing my phone into the pocket of Ian's track shorts. I pause on the aft deck to dig through my duffel bag, but the phone isn't there.

"Shit." I stand up and pat my boobs, my front and back pockets and try to think. Wait. I stuffed my phone into my pocket as I was leaving the hotel. And then in the cab…oh shit. It must have fallen out of Ian's shorts while in the cab.

"Gah!"

I spin around to check the dock, and the cab has already left. And of course, I paid in cash and did not write down the number of the taxi or the driver's name.

"Damn it!"

I'll have to use Find My Phone once I meet up with the crew.

Closing my eyes, I will myself to remember the name of the cab company. Something tells me, though, that I'm shit out of luck, and I'll have to get a new phone.

Brody, my brother, will be okay until then. This morning, I sent a thumbs up to his "good luck" text. If there's an emergency, he knows the boat's name and the captain's name. But knowing my younger brother, the classic second child, he won't consider it an emergency unless our house explodes into a million pieces.

It's fine. Everything is fine.

And then, I look up and take a good long look at this vessel. The Carpe Diem. I've seen her out on the water while I'd worked other yachts, and I always thought she was lovely. Up close, she's an absolutely gorgeous white boat. The windows and the chrome fixtures gleam in the morning sun. The sea beyond the harbor is a brilliant blue and smooth as stone. I'm starting a new job in one of the most beautiful places on earth, and I'm about to make a metric ton of money in wages and tips. Life is good.

I blow out a breath. It's all going to work out for the best.

Feeling exhilarated from all that sprinting, I have nothing but positivity coursing through me.

"Are you my new mommy?"

I whirl around to see a tall, long-haired redhead with legs that won't quit. Juno. I've worked with her before, and relief floods through me as she drops her bag and hugs me tight.

"Weirdo. And yes. Will you be my second?"

"Abso-fucking-lutely!"

And now, I've got my dream second stew.

There's nothing that could possibly ruin this charter season. Not even a lost phone. Life is good, and I'm ready to work.

Chapter Four

Ian

IT DOESN'T OCCUR to me until I'm on the plane, over the Atlantic, headed back to Chicago, how badly I've messed up.

I don't have Vanessa's last name.

I don't know the name of the yacht.

I don't even know the name of the staffing agency. What's the point of having all this money if I can't pull strings? But first, I have to actually have a string.

Who needs an airplane when I can kick my own ass all the way to O'Hare?

My plane lands in the private section, where my family's driver greets me. Seeing Ken brings back the entire reason that I'm here. Sad reasons. A whole lifetime of memories comes flooding back.

"Ken," I say, shaking his hand.

Ken looks drawn and pale. "Sorry we have to see each other like this, kid."

I can't speak. I just nod. Ken rests a hand on my shoulder, and I swallow down the urge to cry in front of this man. I don't know why I resist; he's known me since I was 14.

Numbly, I slide into the front seat. Unusual, but Ken doesn't say a word about it. Thankfully, he doesn't try to make small talk on the way to the hospital. I ask about his family, and thank god, he latches onto that, filling me in on everything I missed.

My sister falls into my arms as soon as I see her at Northwestern University Hospital's cancer center. The next few days will be a blur of activity, but Betsy and I hold vigil at Hollis's bedside for now.

"Inpatient hospice is coming today to fill out some paperwork. I don't think I can…" she starts. She doesn't finish.

The lead doctor then comes in and briefs us about all the things that are about to happen. That Hollis can hear me, that he might squeeze my hand but that it's not a sign that he's getting better. He might rally, he might not.

Betsy looks up at me. "I think he has been waiting for you. You might need to tell him you're here and that it's … that it's okay to go."

Everyone's words sound like I'm underwater. Everything I see looks like a nightmare.

"Sis," I say. "I can't tell him that. But whatever you need, whoever you need me to talk to. I'll handle it."

Betsy grips my hand. "He's suffering. The decline happened so fast. The meds are just keeping him calm, but he's holding on. The two of you are the most bullheaded people I know, so it's down to you."

At my friend's bedside, I hold his hand, so much smaller and weaker than the man I know. Hollis is in there somewhere.

"Hey, buddy. It's me. Ian. Don't worry, I'm not gonna get all sappy. You and I are better on paper than with the face-to-face emotional stuff. But I am gonna hold your hand, so you'll have to deal with that, all right?"

The smallest of squeezes. That's all it takes, and then my mind shifts. This is all real. It's not a nightmare. I'm not going to wake up.

But he needs me. Betsy needs me.

I sit like that for I don't know how long. Me on one side, Betsy on the other. Occasionally, people come in with food, flowers, coffee, and who knows what else. Old friends. Cousins. Uncles. A chaplain. The room is hushed all day as people come in and go out, one and a time, to say goodbye to Hollis. I had pictured this moment a million times, and I thought I'd hate it. The truth is, it's worse than I'd imagined, but I'm glad that I'm here.

The only thing that clues me into it being nighttime is that the visitors stop coming. And still, we sit. We wait. We talk to Hollis, and we talk to each other about Hollis. We share memories of the good times, and I hope he can hear them.

The faintest glimmer of sunrise appears on Lake Michigan through Hollis' hospital room window. Betsy has fallen into a light doze in her chair, and I let go of Hollis's hand to walk over and cover her with a blanket.

His slow, shallow breath becomes even more labored when I return to my post. So much so that Betsy wakes with a start.

As if she hadn't been in a partial dream a second ago, Betsy looks at me and says, "It's time, Ian."

God, what do I say? I have no flowery words. I'm not a guy who prays. But I feel like It's best to send him out on something familiar. A memory.

"Hey, Hollis. Get your shit together; it's time for the fireworks."

The tiniest movement flickers in his eyes. He remembers. "That's right, buddy. I got the coolers filled with Bud Lights, and we're taking the Jeep. Ken's already set up blankets for us down by the Pritzker. It's gonna be the best Fourth ever. Don't you fucking make us late again and miss the opening band like you did last year."

A slight, almost undetectable squeeze, and then his breathing falters. The faintest remaining spark in Hollis' eyes dims, and something beeps on the machines.

"Oh, Hollis," Betsy croaks.

"Bets." I let go of my friend and hug my sister, then let her have a moment alone with Hollis.

I go to the bathroom and quietly vomit the small rations I was able to eat last night.

Wiping down my face and rinsing out my mouth, I look in the mirror.

Hollis and Betsy had a beautiful life together, but it wasn't enough.

There was nothing I could have done to make it last any longer. My money can move heaven and earth, but I can't keep Hollis alive.

And here I am, having met the one—yes, I'm sure she's the one—and I have no idea where she is.

I look in the mirror. I think the fuck not. You are Ian fucking Przinsky. You don't give up because of a little lack of information.

Who knows if ghosts are real, but I swear to god it's Hollis looking back at me now, and I can practically hear his voice.

"You're gonna find this girl, and you're gonna marry her. And don't be a moron about it."

Chapter Five

Vanessa

THE CHARTER SEASON started with a bang.

Literally.

The first week saw us catering to literal royalty. It was wild. The king of a tiny Mediterranean country I'd never heard of before had booked an entire week for his youngest daughter's 23rd birthday celebration. This dinner was supposed to have ended with that princess's prearranged marriage.

Turns out that's kind of a pattern with this particular monarchy.

Our deckhand, Abel, learned what was happening and hatched a plan to marry the princess instead.

After everything that had played out, our crew hadn't expected a tip. But we did get a pleasant farewell surprise from the princess's older sister before the royal family sailed off into the sunset.

And now, back in Monaco to pick up our second

charter of the season, I can breathe for a minute. The bosun, a Bahamian named Elijah, uses his phone to locate mine. I've tried calling every cab company in the entire city of Monte Carlo, but no driver has found my phone.

"I can't believe Abel," Elijah says as we walk down the dock, following the signal. "I told him if I caught him sneaking to the princess's room a second time, I'd have to report him to the captain. I never thought the captain would be privy to all these shenanigans."

I murmur in agreement, waiting for any updates on my phone's location.

Elijah sighs. "And now I'm a man short unless the captain can get me another deckhand."

I see the chef, a Russian named Maksim, standing like a sentinel down the dock, his arms folded, his back to us. Since he finished cleaning the galley, he's been in that same spot all morning. Just watching the street or the boats going in and out.

I gesture toward Maksim with my chin and say to Elijah, "And that one. The way he and Juno are at each other's throats on every meal service. If they don't bang and get it over with soon, I worry he might quit also."

Elijah dismisses my worry. "He's not going anywhere."

I don't ask him what this means, and it's enough for me that our bosun speaks with calm authority. I'm just jumpy, this being my first charter as a chief stew.

So far, my half of the crew is holding it together. My second stew, Juno, would make an excellent chief stew one day. My third stew, Star, is…well, the most generous thing I can say is she's got a good attitude.

At the last crew meeting, I was bracing to be chewed out by the captain because of Star's mistakes. A shy young girl from New Zealand who can't be a day over 21, she says she's had experience with five-star service. Still, she can't set the table to save her life, so I've relegated her to the laundry.

But the chewing out from the captain never came. I have no doubt about his abilities. But for a former Navy SEAL, Captain Joe seems to have an unexpected soft side.

"Here it is!" Elijah exclaims, and I jump. "We're literally on top of it."

I look at his phone, and the tiny dot says that my phone is...directly beneath us. Which means it's in the water. How?

"Oh, no. I must have dropped it while running to the boat last week! Dammit!"

Elijah offers to don a wet suit and retrieve it for me, but I tell him not to bother. "It's been underwater for a week. There's nothing that a bowl of rice can do for me now. I'll have to get another phone. I'll add it to my list."

During my shopping trip later that day for provisions, I put off the search for a phone store as long as possible because phone stores are such headaches for me. I'm having too much fun watching Maksim weave through a street bazaar for extra ingredients. Along the way, I pick up trinkets and baubles to add to my tablescapes, which is the most fun part of my job. Anyone can chuck a bunch of sand dollars on the table. I aim for sparkle, eye-catching conversation starters, and romance.

Maksim is decent company but shy and reserved. Polite, professional. He does not like to talk about himself. At all. I find my mind wandering. What would it be like to stroll these charming streets with someone special? Maybe...maybe with Ian. Sure we'd taken turns jumping each other's bones all night. Made great banter. Bonded, even. But we never really had a date.

I purchase a stack of hand-woven scarves to use as table runners. I wonder what Ian is doing right now?

If you really wanted to know that, you'd have a new phone by now. I grit my teeth and head into a nearby mobile store, where I'm told that my previous provider won't release my contacts or my old number. I have to start from scratch.

"I'm so sorry, madame. You will have to cancel your contract with the other provider, and even then, there is no guarantee of the same number."

Crestfallen and frustrated, I accept my fate and purchase a new phone and a new contract.

On the way back to the boat, the first person I call is my brother.

"Brody?"

"Yeah," he replies. "New number, who this?"

"Idiot. I'm calling to tell you that I'm the one with a new number."

"Sis?"

"Gah! You know my voice."

"I'm just yanking your chain. Ha. See what I did there? Anchor chain."

If my brother ever had a serious moment in his life, I might have a heart attack.

I sigh heavily. "So anyway, here's my new number; talk to you after the next charter."

"Wait, aren't you gonna tell me anything? Any drama? Any boatmances yet? Tell me the dirt!"

"You watch too much reality TV," I sigh.

"Ah, you're no fun."

"Well, one of the deckhands left us for the princess of Austero, so that's something, I guess."

"Holy shit!"

"Yeah."

"Where's Austero?"

"Google exists. Love you, Brody. I'm on my way to a meeting with my stews."

As I continue maneuvering the streets with Maksim never far away, I wish even more that Ian was walking them with me.

Maybe we will get the chance someday like we talked about. If I can find the note he left for me with his number on it. I may be a great, organized chief stew, but my bunk is a mess.

After the stew meeting, I take a few minutes to search my cabin, but I can't find the note anywhere. Maybe it flew out of my pocket when I'd dropped my phone. Perhaps it will turn up. Anyway, I don't want to bother Ian if he's dealing with a family emergency. It would feel really intrusive.

From upstairs above my cabin, I can hear Juno and Maksim arguing. Again.

"Get out of my refrigerator," Maksim barks.

"It's not your refrigerator. It's everyone's," I hear Juno reply. "And I'm just unpacking the figs."

"It's too cold in here for figs. Leave them out to ripen."

"No, you leave bananas out to ripen. Leaving figs out will attract ants."

"There are no ants in my galley!"

"There will be with you in charge!"

"I am just trying to get you to leave my fridge, so I don't have to look at your...."

He trails off. What? What does he not want to look at? I'm dying to know.

He must have gestured at her or something because the next thing I hear is Juno storming off. "I can't help it if a grown-ass man can't stop staring at my nipples. Grow up!"

I cover my mouth to stifle a laugh.

I may never have a great romance on this boat. Juno and Maksim, on the other hand. No question.

Chapter Six

Ian

I_F SHE WON'T CALL or text, I'll just have to track her down.

Hollis's funeral lasted for days. Apart from the visitation, service, and burial, there are meals, brunches, and meetings with lawyers. I do my best to support my sister through it all, though I suck at it.

I'm so deep in my own grief and the trauma of seeing him in the way he was before he died. I'm full of regret for things he and I never did. Things we never said to each other.

And now Betsy is here, alone, pregnant, in their house in the suburbs, while happy families with kids and husbands go on with life all around her. Life isn't fair.

"You need to go," she says. It's a week after Hollis has died, and we've finished going through the last of his paperwork. She's decided she wants to leave his clothes and his office exactly how they are, for the moment. I can't blame her for not being ready to put those things away, and I promise to come back when and if she wants to decide about those things.

I've only been home a week, and my phone has been mostly silent. I'm feeling jumpy. Ready to go on a hunt for Vanessa. I need to hold her. Tell her how I feel. But then again, maybe I shouldn't subject her to starting a relationship while I'm barely hanging on, mentally.

I haven't said a word about wanting to leave.

"No, I'm staying to help you out with the baby; help you get the house ready."

Betsy rubs her tummy and turns off the TV. We've been watching a *90 Day Fiancé* marathon and eating more ice cream than should be legal for two people. She squeezes my shoulder. "Listen. Rob and James are moving in, and they will be there to help me get the nursery ready."

The fact that Hollis's brother and his husband will be here to look after her makes me feel better.

"But you'll need a birth partner or whatever."

She makes a retching noise. "God, the last thing I want is my brother going to Lamaze and breastfeeding classes with me. Sorry, you're out. Elise is in."

Her new mom friend she met online. I'm wary, but I trust her judgment.

I shake my head. "Still, I need to be here to support you."

Betsy shakes her head more vigorously. "You will be. When the baby gets here. For now, you need to go and process and…I don't know. Wander. Whatever it is you're itching to do, do it."

I protest again. It is the Midwestern way of things. "I don't know what you're talking about."

She scoffs. "Listen. I know you pretty well, and you've been alternating between catatonic and obsessively checking your phone and pacing. Whoever she is, you should go to her."

Well, shit. Betsy figured it out. Some of it.

"She's...she's not exactly accessible right now."

This is the first time I've spoken to someone I love about the woman I love. It feels freeing. It also feels wrong because she's going through so much shit.

"By 'accessible,' do you mean she's married? Engaged? Dating someone else? Because I swear to god, if you're going after a cheater, I will disown you. I will cut you out of my will, and all of Hollis's vintage vinyl Led Zeppelin will go straight to the baby."

My sister never fails to make me laugh.

"No, that's not it. Her job is really far away, and it's complicated."

"Complicated shit never stopped you before. Go get her and do what you need to do, and I'll see you back here when the baby comes. And introduce the baby to her auntie, maybe."

With uncertainty still over leaving my sister, I book the jet for the next day.

Throughout the packing and traveling, I continue to check my phone, hoping to hear from Vanessa while also contacting everyone I've ever met, even remotely tied to yachting.

"Yeah, I know a Vanessa. She was a chef onboard a catamaran in Mazatlan last year," says my boating fanatic friend Brett.

"Any idea where she might be now?" Turns out, she got married a year ago and has been living in Houston since then. Not the same Vanessa.

I call in a few other favors, contacting other friends who are into yachting but come up short.

It's time to stop bothering my friends and start opening my wallet.

Once I arrive in Monte Carlo, I begin by asking the yachting staffing agencies. But of course, they aren't allowed to tell me anything. I straight-up bribe them to give me anything on any Vanessa they might have on any vessel at the moment, but it's no use.

Searching the internet for ideas gets me nowhere. It's not like I know the first thing about accessing personnel databases, which would be the ultimate creep move. But hell. I made it this far, and I'm desperate.

I'm in Monaco for a week, spending all day walking up and down the docks, thinking about what I should do. Hoping to catch sight of Vanessa on one of the crafts that come and go out of this harbor.

One day, after walking to the end, where the fishing boats dock, I take a break to order some fried fish from a small open-air stand. As I sit down to eat, I strike up a conversation with one of the local fishermen, a forty-some-thing man with a Slavic accent I can't place.

"I see you eating here every day. Staring at the boats. Watching the white boats come and go all day. What's troubling you? You look lost."

Spilling the whole story about Vanessa feels strange. But somehow, confessing all my efforts to find this woman feels good.

The fisherman brushes the crumbs from his beard and stares me down. I wait for him to tell me to go home. To say to me that I'm out of my depth. That chasing a woman in this way is not how to go about finding love.

Finally, he says, "I might know someone who can help you. But it will cost you."

I'm stunned. "How? How can he help?"

The man glances over his shoulder then turns back to

me. "I don't know how he finds things, and I do not ask. Tell me everything you remember, and for the right price, we'll find which boat for you."

Something about this is very messed up. I take another bite of my fish sandwich and think about it while the fisherman gives me the thousand-yard stare.

I swallow, wipe the grease off my fingers. Finally, I nod. "Let's do it."

After telling this near-stranger everything I know, he simply tells me he'll be in touch. How, when, or where? I don't know.

A week later — a week in which I'm climbing the walls of my hotel room, pacing the city, and alternating between grief and desperation — the fisherman shows up out of nowhere while I'm eating breakfast alone at a sidewalk cafe near my hotel.

He pushed a file folder to me. "In here are the crew lists for every yacht larger than 100 meters that has docked between here and Nice in the last thirty days."

I flip through the pages, and a rock drops into my stomach. "These…these are personnel files. These are copies of drivers' licenses, social security numbers, tax ID numbers. How? Who the fuck are you?"

"You have the money? If not, I'll take the file."

"You'll get your money when I find her."

I flip quickly through the stack, feeling dirty that I have access to sensitive information about so many people at my fingertips. It makes me want to vomit. This is what money can do. No, that's not it. This is what fuck-you money can do. Holy shit. About halfway through the stack, there she is, in photocopies of her driver's license and passport photos. My Vanessa.

I pull the sheet and look. "The Carpe Diem. Slip 19. And it's scheduled to pick up a new charter guest tomorrow in Porte De Fontvieille. That's my chance. I've found her. I don't know what you had to do to get this, but thank you."

"You can thank me with the money," the fisherman reminds me.

"Of course." I hand over the stack of bills, and he pulls the slip of paper away from me.

"What are you doing?"

"You may take a photo of it, but you can't keep the sheet."

"Why not? What are you going to do with it?"

"The answer to that question will cost you something you are not prepared to pay."

A chill runs down my spine, but I cough up everything we agreed on. I make sure to capture the name of the travel agent that books that particular yacht.

I don't know how to end this conversation, so I offer him a croissant and coffee. He hesitates and glares at me. Then he shrugs, takes one of the croissants, and stalks away.

My heart hammers and I can't sit still. I'm elated, and I can't remember the last time I could honestly use that word to describe what I'm feeling.

I have work to do. I have yacht guests to bump. I have phone calls to make. I have clothes to pack. And I have to find an engagement ring.

Chapter Seven

Vanessa

THE SECOND CHARTER goes relatively smoothly, except for
Maksim having a near-meltdown. He and Juno were
having trouble communicating during the first charter. On
the second, a short trip that takes us out to sea between
leaving Monte Carlo and arriving in Porte De Fontvieille,
the bickering is fully operatic.

During dinner service one night, I was prepared to fix
a rejected salad myself without alerting Maksim. But Juno
grabbed the plate and marched to the galley. "The primary
says the kale hasn't been massaged enough to absorb the
dressing."

Maksim had spoken low and calmly but with a lethal
warning. "You feed them that salad. It is perfect."

Juno had lifted an eyebrow at him. "No. I want to see
you massage it. This is fun."

Maksim took a step closer to her and said, "You tell the

primary I can give him a special Russian neck massage that will put him right to sleep."

Juno had scoffed. "What, are you like an ex-hitman or something? That's adorable."

"Get this salad out of my sight!"

At that point, our newest deckhand had to hold Maksim back from the main salon. Juno laughed it off, but I seriously thought he might have marched out there and thrown the primary overboard.

We manage to make it through to the end of the charter with no guests running away with any staff. But after our tip meeting, something changes. Although I'd been devouring Maksim's crew mess meals with a vengeance the first week, something is wrong by the end of the second week.

Sitting in the crew mess, everything smells and tastes rancid. So bad, I have a chat with the captain.

Captain Joe, of course, sticks up for Maksim. To his credit, though, he follows me down to the crew mess to taste for himself.

"Tastes fine. Great, even. Elijah?"

Elijah is no help and rubs his tummy. "I'm sorry, did I eat too many chicken and goat cheese nachos? No, come to think of it, I'm not sorry. It was…" He mimics a chef's kiss and sighs. "We are a lucky, lucky crew. I don't know where he came from, but thank the gods of the sea."

I narrow my eyes at him and try to determine if this is just a bunch of men sticking up for each other or if there is something wrong with me. Juno passes through the crew mess then, and I grab her arm. "Taste those crab cakes and tell me your honest opinion."

I know she'll tell the truth. She can't stand Maksim at the moment. Taking one and popping it into her mouth, her eyes roll back in her head. "Oh my god. He may be a hotheaded jackass, but the man can cook. Damn."

She says all this through a mouthful of food.

Am I being punked?

I wave it off, chalking it up to an unexpected bout of seasickness. "My period is coming," I say to the captain. "My taste buds are off."

"Can I get you anything?" Captain Joe might be older and saltier than the rest of us, but he's a good human.

I laugh and am about to tell him what kind of chief stew would I be if I didn't provision this ship properly with feminine products. Still, I feel a strong need to retch all of a sudden.

I cover my mouth and dash to the head.

"WHAT IS GOING ON WITH YOU?"

Juno's arms are crossed, and her face is resolute.

I move my hand away from my face, where it's been briefly covering my mouth and nose because of the smell wafting from the fishing boat that's just dropped off a load of seafood. "I don't know!"

"Well, chief, you're seriously off your game or on drugs. Either way, we are overdue for a conversation, so let's chat."

This girl is the only person I outrank who I would let talk to me this way.

Juno and I are sitting on the aft deck the day before the next charter guest arrives in Porte De Fontvieille, and had initially been going over the list of plans for the theme parties.

"That fishing boat was really pungent, that's all," I say.

She scoffs. "Bullshit. That's never bothered you before.

Something is up with you. You're not yourself. Is it anxiety? Are you getting ill? Something else?"

I don't think it's anxiety. The tips have been good, and the last charter gave us great feedback. I don't have a history of clinical anxiety. I ask for some examples.

"First of all, you think food tastes off when it doesn't. Then there's the snapping. You told Star to pull her shit together and look up how to make a frozen margarita because you can't hold her hand every time. Which is true, but you were way harsh and told her to get her head out of her ass. That's not like you."

"True," I say.

"And the seasickness. God, I've never seen you throw up, not once in however many seasons of yachting together."

"Also true, I have an iron stomach."

"And yesterday, I bumped into your boobs with the laundry basket, and you got tears in your eyes."

Yes, that happened, but she'd been moving very fast with that basket, and the impact was sudden.

"Do you get where I'm going?"

"I do. But I can tell you I'm not on any medication, not on any drugs, and I've not been drinking on the yacht."

"No, bitch, you need to take a pregnancy test."

Details from the last week begin to swirl into my brain, but then slowly, they stop swirling and click into place.

I look back on everything that's been wrong with me this yachting season. The uncharacteristic seasickness, the food and smell aversions followed by intense, unusual cravings, irritability, sleeplessness, tender breasts.

No. No, I refuse to believe it.

But the diaphragm.

Oh god. I had totally forgotten to stop at the pharmacy in my rush…and after that, I put it out of my head.

"I need a pregnancy test."

Juno raises an eyebrow. "You think?"

"We have so much work to do I don't know if I can go onshore to get one—"

Juno holds up a palm in a gesture to stop me from saying any more. "We have some in the cargo hold."

"How?"

"I'm gunning for your job, lady. I think of everything."

I look at Juno, and I already see it. She's got the know-how, she's got the passion, and she's got the drive. She's quick on her feet and makes drinks faster than anyone I've seen. She'll make an excellent chief stew one day. Maybe sooner rather than later.

I bite my lip and look up at her sheepishly. "Will you come with me and wait with me while I take the test?"

She reaches over and takes my hand. "Let's go."

WHEN WE LINE up to greet the next charter guests on the aft deck, the captain has an announcement.

"This is unprecedented, but it seems that we have a change in plans. Our guest this week canceled suddenly, and another one booked in his place immediately. I don't know the circumstances, and I don't know why, but I've been assured that the new guest won't have any special diet restrictions."

This is unusual. But I've got more significant issues to deal with. First of all, I'm pregnant.

Yes. The little pink double lines showed up on the stupid stick I peed on. And Juno is the only one who knows.

And of course, I can't find Ian's number when I have a real reason to call him.

I'll just have to figure it out the next time we dock.

I nudge Maksim. "No vegans this week. You dodged a bullet."

He snaps his gaze to me. "What did you say?"

He looks so strangely paranoid all of a sudden, I don't know how to respond.

Out of the corner of my eye, I see someone approaching the dock. My knees buckle.

Juno on one side of me props me up.

"Are you okay?" Juno whispers.

I shake my head, then nod.

"Ian. It's Ian," I whisper.

"Who's Ian?"

My mouth dries up, and I point to my middle. Her eyes widen in understanding.

"You can't be serious!" Juno exclaims. The entire crew turns their heads toward us.

But then, it's too late. Ian is coming up the gangplank.

I simultaneously rejoice and curse inwardly.

Things are about to get real interesting.

Chapter Eight

Ian

SHE'S NOT WELL. Vanessa's cheeks have lost their color, and she has dark circles under her eyes.

I have to tamp down the urge to dart past the captain and the scary chef, scoop her up, and take her straight below deck to her bunk. Better yet, take her back to my suite in Monte Carlo, where I can pamper her properly.

But I have to play it cool, no matter how serious I am about claiming her for myself. I don't want to scare her away; she's going to be scared enough because I've just located her by use of some seriously sketchy people.

I'm not proud that I paid people to get access to her. I'm pretty sure some of my money went to the Russian mafia to get the crew manifest of every charter white boat scheduled to make berth in Western Europe this summer season.

Finally, I've found her in Porte De Fontvieille.

I shake hands with the captain, my insides reeling as I can see that Vanessa is close from the corner of my eye.

I'm going to hug her so tight, and I don't care what anyone thinks. If the chef doesn't kill me with this hand-shake, holy cow.

"Vanessa."

She tenses up and shoves her hand in mine before I can go in for the hug. Her jaw is tight, her eyes fierce. I get the message; she doesn't want anyone to know that we know each other.

"Vanessa will take you on a tour of the boat while the guys will bring in your luggage," Captain Joe informs me.

"I'll have the water toys ready for you as soon as you complete the tour of the vessel," the bosun Elijah informs me.

I doubt I'll be using any of those things. Still, I accept the champagne from the second stew, a flame-haired Australian woman named Juno.

Vanessa turns to me as soon as Juno heads downstairs to the galley to check on lunch. "Everything okay with your family?"

I smile. "Yes. No. My friend Hollis… was terminal. He was my sister's husband, and he passed. The funeral was last week. I was prepared but … also not. You know?"

She covers her mouth. "I'm so, so, so sorry, Ian."

"Thank you."

I see the beginnings of tears in her eyes, but, under-standably, she fights them away and takes a few practiced breaths.

The door to the main salon is propped open behind her, and she gestures for me to follow her through.

"I don't understand. Why aren't you at home still? With your sister?"

I'm about to tell her everything Betsy said. But a dark-haired, tattooed deckhand is walking by with my suitcase at that exact moment.

When he moves through and disappears downstairs, I reach out to touch Vanessa's arm.

"My sister practically tossed me out of the house; she was so tired of my fussing. I—"

Captain Joe strides in, not so subtly keeping an eye on Vanessa. She clears her throat. "In here, you have the indoor lounge. You'll want to come here if we're experiencing swells because the higher you are, the less seasick you will feel."

"Vanessa," I try again, reaching for her.

"I'm sorry," she says as the captain leaves the premises. "This is not how our next meeting was supposed to go. I want to hug you, but I can't. And I'm just so shocked to see you…how did you find me?"

I consider lying, but that would be a terrible beginning to a real relationship. I blurt it all out, which perhaps also is a bad idea. "I paid some dark web people to hack the personnel files on the employment agency website."

Vanessa rears back, blinking.

I fucked up. I realize that.

But I'm here now, and I intend to never let her out of my sight again. "I didn't hear from you, and I couldn't get you out of my mind. Would you rather have waited until the end of the season to see if we might run into each other again in some other circumstance? Just let nature take its course?"

She shakes her head, lips tight, and eyes wide and earnest. "No. I mean, maybe. I'm just not sure I want to tell you some things if those are the people you associate with."

"Tell me what?"

I wait and hold my tongue. I want Vanessa to speak

freely. I want to know everything that's going on in that head of hers.

"That I…"

I wait and listen.

And then, the moment passes because we're interrupted by Juno.

"Vanessa, I'm so sorry, I was going to wait until you concluded the tour, but the chef is asking about lunch," the red-haired steward says.

And just like that, Vanessa switches on her professional face. Smiling to her eyes, she graciously turns from Juno to me.

"The original primary had ordered a Grecian feast for one p.m. But we can accommodate whatever you like."

I tell Juno to tell the chef that I'm at the mercy of his whims this week.

"Are you sure? Because I can make him do whatever I want. I mean…I can have him cook whatever you like," Juno says.

I catch the cutting of the eyes from Vanessa to Juno, who shrugs and says, "You know what I meant."

I'm sure I don't want to know any other meaning behind the words she's just said. "Tell him to cook whatever he wants. I'm a big eater so keep it coming."

Juno dashes off, leaving Vanessa alone with me.

"You've made Maksim one happy chef. He might ask you to marry him after this season we've had so far," Vanessa says.

"That's too bad for him because there's only room for one wife in the primary suite."

Vanessa rubs a palm against her forehead and closes her eyes. "You shouldn't say things like that."

I nod, examining her face for any sign of the amazing girl I spent the night with over a month ago.

She's there, somewhere. I can feel her in the air between us.

But I have to stop making her uncomfortable. This isn't how it's supposed to go. "Why don't we finish the tour?"

She provides me with a whirlwind tour of the boat's salons, main deck, the sky deck, the dining area, and we end up last of all in my cabin, where the crew has already stowed my belongings.

My suite for the week is a vast room with white-on-white everything. It takes up the entire width of the ship, with windows on both sides. Modern art pieces on the walls in white, with concealed light fixtures behind them, cast a glow on the walls. The tables, the bathroom fixtures, everything is white marble, white painted wood. The only splashes of color are the nautical pillows on the bed. Oh, the bed. It's wider than a standard king. I run my hand along the softest duvet I've ever felt.

"It's a beautiful room," I say. "When you do get a break because I want you to meet me here."

"I think bedrooms have gotten us into enough trouble."

"Trouble? Vanessa, what does that mean? It was the most incredible night of my life."

She nods but looks sad. I need to know what is happening because she's definitely holding something back.

"It was so wonderful, Ian. But I'm not allowed to fraternize with the guests on charter."

This makes me laugh. "Fraternizing with you is the only thing I came here to do."

"Not unless you want me fired," she says, shaking her head ruefully. "We only just now replaced a deckhand who left with a charter guest. We've had enough upheaval for one season."

"Surely you can sneak down here tonight and have a

midnight snack with me. Totally innocent. Milk and cookies, that's it," I urge.

Vanessa smiles shyly. "That does sound good. I've been craving Oreos like you wouldn't believe."

"Got any in the pantry?"

"Sadly, no. Nowhere to be found on land, either. I checked everywhere during my last provisioning trip," she says.

"Then I'll figure something out. Just promise me. Midnight. After everyone's in bed. Meet me here, and let's talk."

Vanessa smiles softly, touches her earpiece, and looks to the side, her body stiffening. "Yes, Captain."

I watch her shoulders relax again as she listens to whatever the captain is saying in her ear. Blowing out a breath, she says. "Be right there, Captain."

She tells me the captain has invited me to visit the bridge if we're done with the tour.

"Not quite done," I say, brushing her hair and tucking it behind her ear.

"Ian."

"Vanessa."

I give her ample time to run away. She doesn't move a muscle. We stare at each other for what feels like an eternity, and for a small moment, it's just us.

"May I please kiss you, Vanessa?" I say, my voice shaking.

Her brow relaxing, she answers with a small, quiet "Yes. Just one kiss."

Angling my face, I circle her waist and pull her close to me. Our lips meet in a soft, sultry kiss. With my eyes closed, all I can feel are her warm lips; all I hear is our kissing and the faint chatter of the crew in her earpiece.

I let her pull away first. When she does, I see the promise in her eyes, mixed with worry and sadness.

"We'd better go see the captain," she says.

But she's not getting away from me that easily. "Wait. Before you turn into professional Vanessa, you have to tell me what's wrong?"

She smiles tightly and nods. "Tonight. Midnight. I'll meet you."

With another sweeping kiss to my cheek, she takes my hand and leads me up the stairs to meet the captain.

I don't know what's going on with her, but I'm going to find out. And whatever it is, I intend to completely obliterate any of those problems between us. Even if I have to force her off this boat so we can be together.

Either she's going to quit, or I'm going to apply for a job. Both scenarios are fine with me.

Chapter Nine

Vanessa

SLOWLY, quietly, I descend the steps to Ian's cabin, holding my breath. I don't think anyone saw me. In case they do, I made sure to carry a tray of midnight snacks and tea. A cover story. "Mr. Przinsky requested a midnight snack, and I didn't want to wake the chef, so I just took care of it," is my practiced speech.

No matter how big these yachts are, we are always found out. Our crew members' quarters are arranged like spoons in a drawer. Yes, we have bathroom privacy, but the bulkheads are little more than particle board, or it seems like that sometimes. Bunkmates know each other's every move. Fortunately, Juno wouldn't rat me out. Still, it's difficult to sneak around at night without someone, somewhere on this boat, hearing you.

I raise my hand to knock on the door, but it opens before my knuckles can graze the polished wood. I suck in a breath when I see Ian standing in the open doorway, his eyes blazing, his hair damp and clinging to his scalp. The scent of soap pours off his, and I feel a tug inside my body. He's shirtless, clad only in flannel pajama bottoms that sit low on his hips, his vee lines arcing downward as if daring me not to look at the bulge. Ian's chest is pink from the shower and radiates heat.

I want to go to him. I want him to hold me against him and share that scent, the heat. My mind transports back to our one and only night together, and the moment we shared in the shower. We had a lot of moments, but that one was delightful. He'd kissed me so slowly while the steam built around us in that marble stall. So slow, so attentive. So…everywhere. Not a patch of my skin had been left neglected by his lips, tongue, and teeth. Ian had made me feel so treasured. So fucking wanted.

I knew he would do it all over again right now if I asked.

But we need to talk first. And, shit, I need to make sure he's not a freaking mob boss or something. I don't want my baby anywhere near that.

"Hi," I say, and that's all it takes to cause Ian to blink and for his mouth to spread into a wide, relieved smile.

Without another word from either of us, he slips one arm around my hips and pulls me into his room. He pivots and firmly closes the cabin door.

He angles his face and captures my lips in his, and I want to get lost in the moment. His soft lips belie his power to ensnare me. I could easily let go and let him have his way. I want that. So bad. I've missed him so much.

He deepens the kiss after only a second's pause for air, slipping his tongue into my mouth. The feel of his arms around me, that warm, scented skin pulling me into that little world where it's just him and me.

Pregnant. You're pregnant, and you need to tell him. Now.

I gather every ounce of strength and pull back from the kiss. "Stop. Wait."

He backs off right away but looks confused. Then, he laughs. "The tray. I'm so sorry. I'm going to make you drop it, aren't I? Here." He takes the small platter and sets it down on a side table laden with a crystal vase of fresh gardenias. I take that moment to gather my wits, though my eyes travel over the backs of his shoulders, his shoulder blades. I have to close my fists to keep myself from running my fingers over those delightful bumps and ridges.

He turns back to me and reaches for me, smashing our bodies together so tightly that the rise and fall of my chest presses me closer to him. "Now, where were we?"

"We need to talk," I say.

He pauses halfway to the kiss and arches an eyebrow. "That sounds like the beginning of a breakup."

"We're not officially together; how can I break up with you?"

Something flashes across his face, but he locks it up tightly in the next second. What was it? Sadness? Surprise? A combination of both. Whatever it was, it's gone and replaced by that charming smirk. "Call this what you want. But you're my girl."

"You might not say that after I tell you what I need to tell you."

His face doesn't register a single concern or worry. His expression only communicates contentment. With his arms wrapped around me, his hands covering my whole back, he looks as if there's nothing to fear at all.

"I'm being serious, Ian."

His sandy eyebrows knit together.

"So am I. Whatever you have to tell me? Don't worry. It won't matter; it won't affect our future because I'm with you one hundred percent. That's why I'm here. That's what I came to tell you. I needed you to know that I will track you down no matter where you go. You'll never get rid of me. And yeah, I fucked up by digging up your employment information, but that's it. It was just one time, and I don't owe money to anybody. I'm never dealing with those people again. I promise. Do you want to keep working on yachts? Fine. I'll be there, and I'll buy up every charter."

I laugh. "You can't buy up every single charter."

He considers this for a second. "You're right. That would be extremely inefficient. I'll buy up all the charter yachts."

"There goes my career."

He looks me over and kisses my forehead. "You look different. I can't figure out what it is."

He's so goofy and sweet and messy; I just want to cry. Is this the person I want to raise a baby with? I like him so much, but he's so intense. He's so all over the place; he's not ready for a baby, wife, or girlfriend. He might think he is, but I just don't know.

But the bottom line is he needs to know the truth.

"Ian," I whisper because my voice has left me.

The captain chooses that moment to interrupt in my earpiece. "Vanessa, Vanessa, Joe. Can you come to the bridge, please?"

Ian's grip on me tightens. "You've gone suddenly pale. Are you ill?"

I shake my head. "It's the captain. I have to go."

"We're not done talking."

"You don't understand; I have to answer when the captain calls me."

In my earpiece, Captain Joe's gravelly voice raises. "Vanessa, Vanessa, are you on the radio? Please come to the bridge."

"I'm here, Captain," I say, pressing the earpiece button. "I'm just not quite awake. I'm on my way."

I look apologetically to Ian. "I gotta go."

Ian looks disappointed. "You said you have to tell me something important."

I don't want to blurt out the news like this and then walk away. We need to have a whole conversation. It would not be fair.

I lean over and kiss him on the nose, but he takes more. Warmth floods my veins and moisture pools in my panties. Even with the captain breathing down my neck, Ian can make me ready to crawl all over him and stick my tongue down his throat. Our tongues tangle together as my radio squawks in my ear. "That's funny because it sure as hell looks like you were awake on the monitor five minutes ago, or so I've been told."

Everything clicks together. Someone saw me on the monitor and woke up the fucking captain. Who would do that? Surely not Maksim. He doesn't seem the type to stick his nose into other people's personal business.

"On my way."

I'm so fucked. Now Captain Joe is about to see me leave the guest's cabin when I'd already said I was on my way.

I kiss him one more time and pull away from him. "Buckle up. I'm about to get fired, and then we'll have plenty of time to talk. On the dock."

I leave Ian despite his protests, and I ignore the sounds of his cursing and attempts to follow me.

"If you're in trouble, then I'm here to help. Nobody is firing you. I won't allow that to be on your employment record."

None of that will matter if I have to quit working on charters because I'm pregnant. It's not like I'm going to leave a baby with a nanny for months at a time. Or any age child for that matter. I'm sure there's a way to do it, but I can't.

I climb the steps to the control bridge, every carpeted step another step closer to the end of my yachting career.

I smile ruefully as I enter the bridge and see Captain Joe standing there with his arms crossed over his bare chest. Next to him is Dustin, one of the deckhands smiling gleefully. On the last charter, I had reported him to the captain for sharing a midnight hot tub session with one of the guests. Ever since Abel left and Dustin didn't get the lead deckhand job, he's decided he no longer cares about the fraternization rules when it comes to himself. But he's been waiting for me to fuck up. Easy enough to spot me on the bridge monitor while on anchor watch. Shit.

"Hi, Captain," I say, my face stoic as he gestures for me to have a seat.

Here it comes. The end of my career.

I'm never going to work in yachting again because my stupid heart couldn't say no.

Countless deckhands and crew members have gotten away with kissing, flirting, and even sleeping with guests.

But that's the story of my life, isn't it?

Steal one piece of candy from the store and get caught.

Have one one-night stand and get pregnant.

I wonder when I'll learn my lesson?

Chapter Ten

Ian

VANESSA STANDS behind me to my left, gracefully sets the plate down, and lifts the cloche. Steam billows out, the scents of this five-star dinner wafting through the air.

I was relieved that Vanessa did not get fired for our little meet-up last night; the captain bought the midnight snack cover story, hook, line, and sinker.

"Grilled sea bass with a raspberry orange reduction and fresh, local escargot—"

She stops short. The captain glances up past my shoulder, and I turn to look at Vanessa.

Her eyes are wide, and her hand covers her mouth.

"Excuse me, I'm so sorry," she apologizes through the hand, muffling her words.

Without further explanation, she bolts to the interior, nearly knocking over Juno, who's on her way to refill my wine glass.

"Van?"

Juno looks at me and then at the captain. "What happened? Is she sick?"

The captain shrugs but looks concerned. "I have no idea." Captain Joe turns to me and apologizes for the chief stew's abrupt exit.

I'm torn between causing Vanessa to lose her job and needing to check on her.

"I've never seen her get seasick before," Captain Joe remarks, standing as if ready to go check on Vanessa.

I glance out to sea, but it's as smooth as can be.

The thought plays in my head. Something Vanessa said when we were together the first time. "I never get seasick."

Things click together in my head. A memory from when my sister was first pregnant. She craved chocolate milk. She would gag at the smell of cooking meat. She looks so pale, like she can't eat or sleep.

Vanessa's pregnant.

Pregnant!

How could I be such an idiot? Of course.

She's been trying to tell me this whole time but didn't know how.

She's scared of what my reaction would be.

Honestly, I don't even know what my reaction is. All I feel is instinct. The need to make her lie down, put her feet up, and let me stuff her full of Oreos or whatever she wants.

"More wine, Mr. Przinsky?" Juno pours, and I nod dumbly. I'm too stunned and overwhelmed with emotion to speak words.

I need to go to her.

"I'm very sorry, Captain; I have to excuse myself."

"Yeah," says Captain Joe. "I figured."

I go to her without another word. Except I don't exactly know which part of the boat she went to.

I run through the salon and down the stairs to the galley.

There, Maksim is stirring something sweet-smelling on the stove. "Where's Vanessa?" I ask him.

Maksim looks up at me, his severe brow drawn together. "Probably in her cabin, tossing her guts up. Again. Are you not going to eat dessert? I made something special."

A sudden idea occurs to me. "Maksim, do you know what Oreos are?"

He gives me a menacing grin. "Yes, I know what Oreos are; they are an American lard sandwich cookie."

"Do you think you could make them from scratch?"

The chef scoffs. "I can make them, yes. I can make them better than store-bought." He crosses his bulky arms. "Is this for wooing a woman?"

"Yes."

"Give me two hours."

"It's not a contest, I just…."

"Two hours!" Maksim shouts at me, and I retreat from the galley.

I check her cabin, but she's not there. I circle around the back deck and finally find Vanessa on the stern on the bottom level, at the swim deck, out of sight of everyone.

"There you are."

I hear a laugh come from her. She turns to me and smiles sadly. "I knew you'd find me."

Sitting cross-legged next to her on the swim deck with a slight groan at the twinge in my muscles, I reply, "It is my new occupation. Finding you wherever you may roam."

Vanessa lets out a long breath. "It seems there's no way around it. I have to tell you the truth. Ian, I'm pregnant."

Chapter Eleven

Vanessa

I WAIT for him to react. I expect horror, quickly masked with understanding and concern, followed by reassurances.

But that's not what Ian gives me.

Instead, he croaks, "Vanessa, I know."

Shock mixed with relief is all I feel at first. "You know?"

He smiles and places a hand over mine, resting on the teak. "Yeah."

"How?"

"You ran off to puke after a whiff of meat; it was just like my sister."

"Your sister?"

"Yeah, she's having a baby in about a month or two. I knew you weren't seasick. Experienced crew members don't get seasick. I knew you said your boobs were sore when I hugged you. And then, the cravings. It all added up."

I shake my head in disbelief that he's figured it out. "I took a test last week, and I swear I was going to try to find you, but I lost my phone, and then because of some stupid local law, I had to get a new number...." I yammer on about my phone situation, hoping that will explain why I hadn't called.

"I knew I'd done the right thing to track you down. Now I have an even better reason to look after you."

"Ian. Don't say that. You don't know if you want to be with me for the long run."

He shrugs. "You took my heart and gave me a baby in return. I mean, if you want to keep it."

"I do want to keep it. But Ian, you can't be serious. You've known me for a day and a half. You can't want to marry me."

"Forty-seven hours, sixty-eight minutes, and twelve seconds."

I shake my head. "You're counting hours? Who does that?"

"I do. Get used to it. I also counted the hours we were apart, which was a very ugly journal entry. You probably don't want to read it. I came to find you, to tell you that I want you to be my wife. What I got instead was a family. Please consider taking on me as well as the baby. I promise to take care of you."

This is too much. Too much, too soon. I need time to think. "You have to get off the yacht in about eleven hours. I have to finish the season, and in the meantime, you're going to go back to the mainland and get cold feet."

He shakes his head and declares, "I'm not going anywhere. Whether you remain on this boat or come away with me, I'm staying next to you."

I can't believe what he's saying. "I can't go away with you. I have responsibilities."

I glance around. "Seems to me your crew can handle it."

"But…"

"The alternative is I apply for a job as a deckie, and I move into your bunk."

"Juno is in my bunk."

"She can bunk with Maksim for obvious reasons."

I laugh. Ian is so ridiculous. Ridiculous and mine. "You can't work on this ship."

"Watch me."

There seems to be no way for me to discourage this madness.

And so, we talk through all of the scenarios. We talk and talk and talk, the only other sounds being the waves against the hull, the distant sounds of people partying on a boat anchored somewhere nearby.

I don't know how much time passes before Ian presents me with a small red square box.

"What is that, Ian?"

He says nothing but opens the box, and inside is a beautiful, delicate ring set with tiny pearls.

"Ian."

"Will you marry me?"

"Ian." I can't stop saying his name, and I keep repeating it; I'm so shocked.

"This is insane. You can't seriously be ready to commit to a wife and a baby."

"What are your plans if I wasn't here?"

"I don't know."

We're in the middle of hashing it out when a massive shadow blocks out the sun. Maksim hovers nearby with a small serving plate in one hand.

He leans over, and on the plate is a perfect little pyramid of Oreo cookies.

"Maksim, what?"

"Oreo cookies. American lard sandwiches. Mine are better."

I pick one up and examine it. "Where did you find these? I haven't seen one in weeks."

"I made them for you."

I sniff them. "This is for real. You actually made Oreos for me?"

"Your fiancé ordered them for you."

Ian interjects. "Well, she hasn't said yes, yet."

I look from Ian to Maksim. "You made cookies for me?"

Maksim nods awkwardly.

I turn to Ian. "I'm saying yes now." I tackle him with a giant hug.

Maksim comments, "Or maybe you should marry me since I'm the one who made the cookies for you."

Ian and I laugh, and I rise to my feet to wrap my arms around Maksim's middle. "Thank you, thank you, thank you!"

Someone behind us clears her throat. I spin around and see Juno standing there. "Um…" she says.

Maksim lets go of the hug and turns to Juno. "I wasn't hugging her; she hugged me."

Juno juts her hip out and lifts an eyebrow. "Why are you telling me this?"

"Because…" Maksim stammers. "Because I don't want you to think I'm going to be giving out hugs everywhere."

"Funny," Juno says. "I thought you were such a hugger until now."

She rolls her eyes and walks away.

I could be mistaken, but I think I hear a distant growl coming from somewhere. I can't tell if it's from Ian or Maksim.

Chapter Twelve

Ian

With Vanessa backed against the cabin door, we are blissfully unleashed.

Vanessa moans into my mouth, and my heart sings. Her breath and her moans are part of me. We kiss and grope each other, her middle arching up against me.

"This feels way less naughty now that everyone knows we're a couple," she whispers with a giggle.

As soon as possible, Juno will be promoted to chief. Then Vanessa and I will settle somewhere she doesn't have to smell seafood for the duration of her pregnancy.

I hate that she has to leave a job that she loves. But we'll talk about that. After.

Firmly, I grip her hips to steady her as I press my pelvis against hers.

Vanessa wraps one leg around my waist, hooking me in even tighter. I feel the heat between her legs, that thin rectangle of fabric covering her sex radiating.

My thick fingers slide the panties aside and sink into her folds. Swollen and red from our kissing, her full lips part in her breathlessness.

"Oh my god, I missed you, Ian." The tremor in her voice stabs at my heart. I hate that she missed me that much, while at the same time, I'm deeply humbled that she was thinking of me. It's strangely gratifying and heart-breaking, making this moment that much sweeter.

"Vanessa, I'm so sorry I didn't tie you to the bed and keep you from going on this fucking yacht in the first place," I breathe.

Her eyes widen as her damp heat reacts to my words and my touch. Her warm honey drenches me. I'm salivating for it.

"T—tell me. How would you stop me? You couldn't."

Punctuating each phrase with a strum against her clit, I answer with eyes on her like she's my prey. "I will do. Everything it takes. To keep my eyes on you."

She bites her lip, whimpering; her sweet juices flow down my fingers.

I am an asshole who wants more and more. More sweetness, more wetness, more of everything. "I would cuff you to the bed. And torture you. With just one…gentle… light finger…all over your body…until you were begging for mercy. And then I would spoil you fucking rotten."

A raspy moan escapes her, her pelvis grinding into my hand. It's not enough.

Falling to my knees, I spread her legs apart and soak those damp panties with my tongue.

Then, I tug them aside with a hooking thumb and bury my tongue inside her folds. I needed this. I need her to feed me, nourish me. I'm going to drink all of her.

Her muscles clamp down, and I feel her release rush through her.

Sweet nectar spills out, the heat of this moment hurtling me closer to nutting in my pajama bottoms.

"Ian. Holy shit."

"I need to be inside you, angel. Now."

My Vanessa spreads for me, and I tug her soaked panties down her legs, allowing her to kick them off. As soon as I come to standing, her legs hook around me in a hurried grip, urging me to take her.

Dropping my pajama bottoms on the floor, I spread her wide and sink my cock into her heat. She throws her head back and hisses, bumping it against the polished wood.

I instinctively cup the back of her head in one hand, protectively. Both of us take one second to stare at each other breathlessly. We've gone to that place where it's just her and me. There is no tomorrow, just us. Just right now.

I sheathe into her heat, piercing her to the hilt and thrusting upward. Her hips rock into me, her sex clamping down tight around me. I see the needful look in her eye as she tells me she wants more.

"You want this cock? It's yours. Grab it. Suck it in. Take it," I grit out.

We could lose our balance like this, but I've got her under control as she bucks and writhes. I pull out and push back in, testing how much she can take.

"Harder," she whines.

Again, I pull out slowly and shove back inside, right where I want to be.

"Good. Harder. Please," she begs.

"Careful, angel, I've got weeks of frustration to take out on you."

She breathes, "Take it out on me. Take it all out."

My teeth bared, one arm bearing all my weight; I take

my Vanessa for a ride. She feels so good against me. Riding my cock, whining, and moaning and whispering my name.

"Yes," she rasps.

"I like that word. That's what I like to hear. Are you gonna say that at the altar?"

I punctuate this question with another thrust.

Her eyes closed, she moans out her answer.

"Eyes on me, angel."

Vanessa's eyes fly open and land on me. "Yes," she says.

"Good girl. Are you gonna say yes to having my baby?"

"Yes."

"Are you gonna stay in bed when I tell you to from now on?"

"Yes, Ian."

"Good girl."

Her body clamps around my cock, and I explode into her, seething out her name. Everything goes black for half a second as I release my seed into her.

My Vanessa. My wife. Mother of my baby.

With her wrapped around me, I take her to the jetted tub in my suite's bathroom. With her in my lap, we sit together and kiss as we wait for the steaming water to rise. I place a soft kiss on her cheeks and both eyelids. "I love you so much."

She smiles. "Thanks for finding me. Thanks for taking the news so well. So unbelievably well. And thanks for the Oreos."

I cage her in between my legs in the tub, so she rests against my chest. I wrap her up in my arms and sigh.

I finally feel normal. The most normal I've felt in forever.

"So, chief stew. Where are we headed tomorrow?"

She hums and traces her fingers over my forearms. "I think I'd like to go to Chicago."

"Chicago? Really?"

Vanessa nods. "If I'm going to be your wife, I'd like to meet your family."

My heart explodes with gratitude. I pull her in close, reaching around to cup her chin in my hand, drawing her in for a kiss over her shoulder.

And then, unexpectedly, like a tornado and a snow-storm, a wave of blackness hits me. Hollis. Hollis isn't going to be there to meet her. Hollis will never meet either of our children. But mine? Mine will grow up with two parents. I can't stand this thought. The tears flow.

The room goes blurry, my throat burns.

"Baby," Vanessa whispers.

I let go of her, resting my head against the tile, pressing my balled fists into my forehead. A heaving sob explodes from me. My eyes tightly closed, I feel her move against me. And then, she has me. She's turned around in the tub and is cleaving us together in a firm hug. Her sweet head rests against my chest, and she remains there until this terrible moment passes.

She waits and waits for me until the water goes cold. Then, she gets up, opens the drain to let out the cold water, and twists the knob to hot again. "Take as long as you need."

I do not deserve her.

By the time she snuggles back into my arms, I've calmed down again, enough that I'm able to talk. "My sister already is looking forward to meeting you," I say, sniffling.

"You told your sister about me?"

"If I hadn't, she would have dragged it out of me."

"She sounds like my kind of girl. I hate the idea of leaving Juno and the rest of the crew."

"I think Juno can hold her own."

"Yes, she can. But I'm going to miss her."

I massage a comforting hand over the slick skin of her back. "I understand."

"Can we actually do this? Start a life together after a one-night stand? Do people do that?"

I press a deep, sensuous kiss to Vanessa's lips.

"People can, and they do all the time."

"Aren't you scared, Ian?"

"I'm not."

"Not even of poopy diapers? I can't picture you handling that."

Squeezing her close, I declare confidently, "Watch me."

Epilogue

A year later

Ian

"Vanessa! So much poop! I lied, and I'm scared!"

Never in my life have I eaten my words with such clarity.

Our son, George, is a tiny, three-week-old baby. And yet I am terrorized by his poops. I have learned the meaning behind the saying, "five pounds of shit in a one-pound bag."

George looks up at me adorably and makes that face that lets me know he's making more where that came from.

I should be thrilled. He's putting on weight, finally. Vanessa was worried for a time when George struggled to latch on after he was born.

Then, she emotionally beat herself up about not producing enough milk.

Fortunately, my sister was there to help convince Vanessa that formula is a perfectly acceptable option and doesn't mean she's failed at anything.

Betsy and Vanessa took to each other right away. Now the six of us, plus Hollis's brother and his husband, all live together in the old family house in the suburbs. It's been dubbed the Home Alone house, with plenty of room for all of us.

It feels good to stay here with this cobbled-together family. The help is excellent, and we both love being there for Betsy. It feels like a constant point on my horizon and makes me see what can be good about staying in one place for a while.

I can do a lot of things. Whatever she's craving, I can feed her as much as she wants. I will go out for root beer floats and Oreos at three a.m. I will rock George back to sleep at all hours so that Vanessa can rest. I can advocate for her with the pediatrician and the lactation specialists. I can even do my best to ensure she knows that her worth is not tied to how successful she is at breastfeeding.

And Vanessa is not running to save me from the horrors happening in the nursery right now. Well, that's fine. She can rest as long as she needs to.

"Guess it's just you and me, kid," I say to my son. Again, his tiny face is trained on me. And for the first time, he smiles. Legitimately, with a wide, toothless grin.

"Yeah, you know what you did," I say, laughing. But I'm also nearly crying because this is the first time my son has smiled at me. He's never wanted anyone but his mother. At this moment, seeing me acting like a helpless fool, he's amused. And he likes me.

I'm so overcome, I don't even care about the literal shit show in his drawers. I hug him close, tromp over to the nursery sink, and start running a bath. Forgetting about the mess on my shirt, we pals have a heart to heart while I clean him up.

"I know. I agree; she's pretty amazing."

He coos and his little arms punch the air.

"Yes. We're going to clean you all up, and then you're going to take a nap, so maybe Mommy and Daddy can nap simultaneously for once. Oh no, it's not your fault." I say when George's chin begins to wobble.

Coming up behind me, Van rests her head on my back and is about to wrap her arms around me from behind. "Stop! George made a mess on my shirt!"

Vanessa looks back at me in the bathroom mirror, over my shoulder in horror. "Oh my god. Here. I got this. Go take a shower."

Moments later, I've cleaned up and am now hanging out in the shower, hoping my favorite person will join me. It's been exactly six weeks since she gave birth, but I haven't asked if the doctor has given Vanessa the all-clear.

I don't want to push until she's ready. Even if all she wants is a fun shower, I'm good.

Never a disappointment, Vanessa soon steps into the steam with me.

"Hi," I say, smiling at her like a dope. "How's the little prince?"

"Napping," she says, a dreamy look on her face. "Which I will be again, soon."

I laugh and playfully nip at her cheekbones, nose, and chin with my teeth. I'll never want to stop playing with her. "You were just taking a nap," I remind her.

Her hand drags over the cheeks of my ass, and she backs me against the wall. "And I will again after my husband ravages me in the shower."

I bite my lip in excitement and glee. "You're good to go?"

She giggles and nods. "I'm good to go."

I look down into her heated gaze. Without breaking eye contact, I hitch one of her legs around my hips and slowly back her against the tile. "Like this?"

My hardened cock slicks through her folds, teasing her.

Vanessa responds by pushing back, grinding against me. Her heat demands more of me, and she's about to get it.

My fingers split her lower lips wide, and I find her taut clit begging for attention. Vanessa's eyes roll back in her head as I work deadly circles around it, every moan from her pushing me closer to the edge. Her cheeks flush intensely pink, and she writhes against my hand, groaning. Her sex seizes against me as she comes.

I seat my cock inside her and pin her to the wall.

"And your diaphragm?" I ask, even as I'm thrusting in.

She gasps, taking all of me, scooting her leg up higher to open up more for me.

"I don't have it. I threw it out."

With another thrust, I rasp: "Good."

Her sweet cunt clasps around my length, and I almost blackout with how good she feels. I missed this.

"I want more."

"You got it, baby," I say, my breath hitching as I thrust deeper.

She laughs. "Yes, that. But I meant more babies. More of…all of this."

I have so many questions, despite how happy I am.

"I thought you wanted to do at least one full summer as a chief stew? I thought you wanted to see Thailand? Tahiti? Spain?"

Smiling wickedly, she replies, "I do. But I made it to chief stew. And I kind of felt like…that was enough. I wanted to see if I could do it, and I did. And…"

I nearly forget what she's been saying because my brain has been frizzle-fried by this ecstasy. This motion within the sweetness of her slick heat, the nearness of my release.

"And?"

Vanessa bites her lip. "And we can just go to Spain when we want to. Right?"

I laugh and, at the same time, explode into her. "Fuck," I growl, nipping her shoulder as my body seizes against hers. "Finally, you see things my way."

Again, she laughs but at the same time clamps her tight muscles around my spent cock. "Whatever makes you most satisfied, you can think that," she teases.

Nothing can satisfy me more than Vanessa, our family, and our home. Wherever we are is home on land or sea. I don't care if I never convince her to see things my way on any other subject. Life on her terms is pretty damn sweet.

THE END

THANK you for reading Secret Baby on Board! If you enjoyed this story, please visit my website at authorabbyknox.com for links to many more titles to read. Follow me there to keep up with my latest releases. While you're there, be sure to sign up for my mailing list to get free content, and be the first to know about upcoming projects.

About the Author

Abby Knox writes feel-good, high-heat romance that she herself would want to read. Readers have described her stories as quirky, sexy, adorable, and hilarious. All of that adds up to Abby's overall goal in life: to be kind and to have fun!

Abby's favorite tropes include: Forced proximity, opposites attract, grumpy/sunshine, age gap, boss/employee, fated mates/insta-love, and more. Abby is heavily influenced by Buffy the Vampire Slayer, Gilmore Girls, and LOST. But don't worry, she won't ever make you suffer like Luke & Lorelai.

If any or all of that connects with you, then you came to the right place.